For Jackie—she and her mother know why

ANN ESTELLE STORIES

Queen of Hearts

BY MARY ENGELBREIT

HarperCollinsPublishers

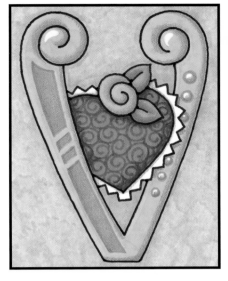

alentine's Day was one of Ann Estelle's favorite holidays.

She liked boxes of chocolate, of course, and candy hearts, and cookies with red sprinkles. And she loved getting valentines from all her friends and family.

But the thing Ann Estelle liked most of all about Valentine's Day was  making things.

Red and pink and white construction paper. Scissors and glue. Ribbons and lace and *lots* of glitter.

es, *Valentine's Day* was definitely one of the best holidays of all.

t school Ann Estelle's class was decorating boxes to hold their valentines. Ann Estelle brought a plain brown shoe box from home. But it wasn't plain for long.

First Ann Estelle cut a slot in the top of The Box for valentines to go in. Then she covered The Box with pink paper. On the front, in her fanciest handwriting, she wrote "the Queen of Hearts."

 valentine box needed lace. And glitter, of course. It needed candy hearts too, and luckily Ann Estelle had some in her craft box.

the Queen of Hearts

But it still looked sort of ...ordinary. And ordinary was definitely not good enough for Ann Estelle's valentine box.

At home Ann Estelle and her friend Gracie had fun playing dress-up. This gave Ann Estelle an idea. Pink feathers would give *The Box* a look of distinction. Sparkling jewels would add a bit of color. Silk roses and daisies would be a nice touch, too.

Ann Estelle squirted the flowers with *her mother's perfume.*

"Wait until I get all this on The Box," said Ann Estelle.

 nn Estelle visited her neighbor Tommy. Playing with his cars gave her another idea. She also remembered a long red-and-white ribbon she had seen in her mother's sewing box.

The next day at school, Mrs. McGilligan said, "My goodness, a Valentine's Day box that *rolls*." It certainly isn't ordinary now, thought Ann Estelle. It's the best box in the entire world.

he next day was Valentine's Day. Ann Estelle's friends stopped by her desk all morning to admire The Box.

"I like the flowers best," said Gracie.

"How 'bout those feathers!" said Audrey Ann.

"Cool wheels," said Michael.

Ann Estelle was so proud she thought she might burst.

Finally, after recess, it was time to pass out the valentines.

And suddenly Ann Estelle didn't feel proud anymore.

She didn't feel happy.

She felt *awful*.

All week long she had worked on The Box. She had cut and glued and taped and sewed. She had made the best box in the entire world—but she hadn't made one single valentine.

How could she have forgotten to make Valentines?!?!

G racie came by Ann Estelle's desk and dropped a valentine into The Box. It was a little hard for her to find the slot among all the feathers and flowers.

the Queen of Hearts

for: ANN ESTELLE

t's the best box I've ever seen," said Gracie. "Aren't you giving away your valentines?"

And suddenly Ann Estelle knew what to do.

"**Y**essiree," she said. "Here's yours."

She pulled a daisy off The Box and handed it to Gracie.

udrey Ann wore her pink feathers in her hair. Michael and Sophie raced the cars that had been wheels for The Box. Mrs. McGilligan tied the red-and-white ribbon in her hair.

hen Ann Estelle got back to her desk, *The Box* was plain again. Only the pink paper was left, and it was ripped and ragged. One big tear went all the way through the words *the Queen of Hearts*. But it was full of valentines from Ann Estelle's friends.

nn Estelle smiled.

"What a **fun** day!" said Gracie.

"This," said the Queen of Hearts, "has turned out to be the best Valentine's Day ever!"

Queen of Hearts
Copyright © 2005 by Mary Engelbreit Ink
Manufactured in China by South China Printing Company Ltd.
All rights reserved.
www.harperchildrens.com

Library of Congress Cataloging-in-Publication Data

Engelbreit, Mary.
Queen of Hearts / by Mary Engelbreit.—1st ed.
p.   cm. — (Ann Estelle stories)
Summary: Ann Estelle is so busy creating the most
beautiful Valentine mailbox in class, she forgets to make cards for
her classmates.
ISBN 0-06-008181-3 — ISBN 0-06-008182-1 (lib. bdg.)
[1. Valentine's Day—Fiction. 2. Valentines—Fiction.
3. Schools—Fiction.] I. Title.

PZ7.E69975Qt 2005   [E]—dc21   2003001823

Typography by Stephanie Bart-Horvath
1 2 3 4 5 6 7 8 9 10
❖
First Edition